A ROOKIE READER®

MESSY BESSEY

By Patricia and Fredrick McKissack

Illustrations by Richard Hackney

Prepared under the direction of Robert Hillerich, Ph.D.

CHILDRENS PRESS®

CHICAGO

To Mom Bess
who is never *a mess*

Library of Congress Cataloging in Publication Data

McKissack, Pat, 1944-
  Messy Bessey.

  (A Rookie Reader)
  Summary: Bessy finally cleans up her messy room.
  [1. Cleanliness—Fiction. 2. Behavior—Fiction]
I. McKissack, Fredrick. II. Hackney, Rick, ill. III. Series.
PZ7.M478693Me   1987   [E]   87-15079
ISBN 0-516-02083-8

Look at your room,
Messy Bessey.

See, colors on the wall,

books on the chair,

toys in the dresser drawer,

and games everywhere.

Messy Bessey, your room
is a mess.

See, shoes on the bed,
coat on the floor,

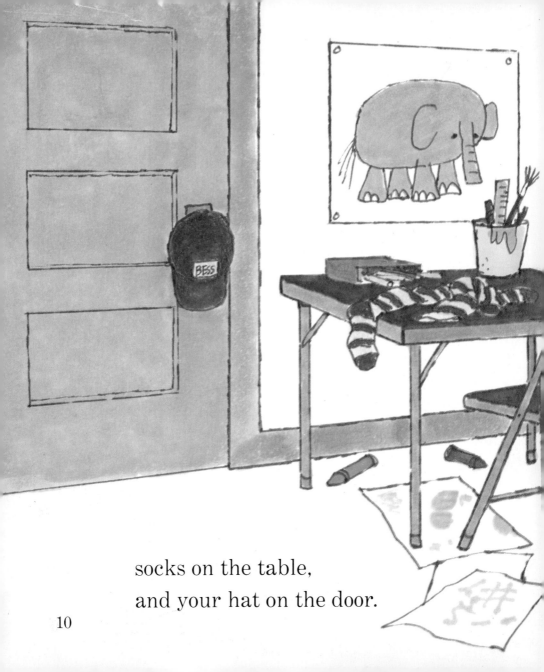

socks on the table,
and your hat on the door.

Bessey look at your
messy room.

See, the cup in the closet,
cookies on the pillow,

gum on the ceiling,
and jam on the door.

15

Messy, Messy Bessey,
your room is a mess.

Get the soap and water.

Get the mop and broom.

Get busy Messy Bessey,
you must clean your room.

So, Bessey rubbed and
scrubbed the walls,

the ceiling,

and the floor.

She made her bed,

picked up her things,

and closed the closet door.

Hurrah! Good for you
Miss Bessey.
Just look at you, too.

Your room is clean
and beautiful . . .

just like you!